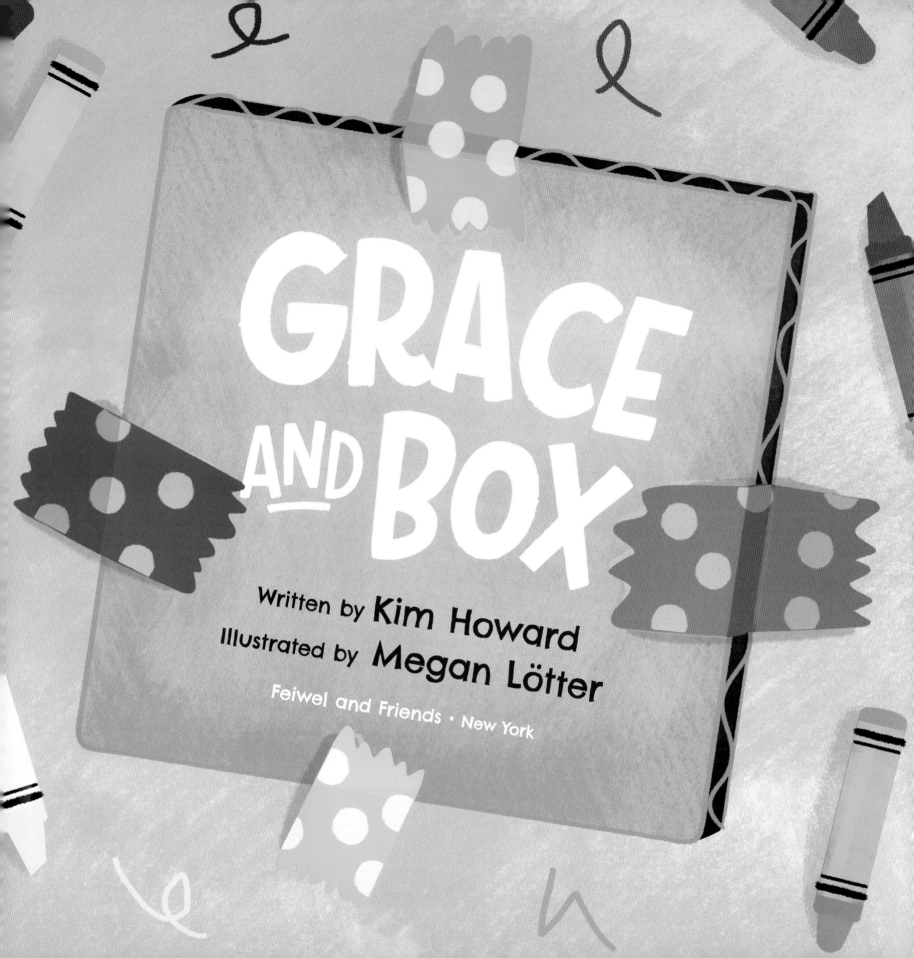

GRACE
AND BOX

Written by **Kim Howard**
Illustrated by **Megan Lötter**

Feiwel and Friends · New York

The day the new refrigerator came,
Grace got Box.

On Monday, Box was a rocket.

On Tuesday, Box was a home.

On Wednesday,
Box was a tent for camping,

and also some ruins in Rome.

On Thursday, Box was a submarine.

On Friday, Box was Hong Kong.

On Saturday,
Box was a deep,
dark tunnel.

But on Sunday,
something was wrong.

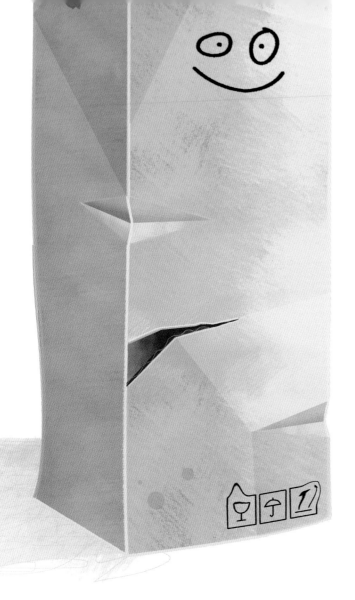

In one corner,
Box was sagging
and one of his walls
had a rip.

One flap on Box
was bent and crumpled.
Box was a sinking ship.

Grace gave him a checkup.
His heartbeat seemed okay.

She let him rest on the couch,
and read him stories all day.

Next, she tried a bandage

and then some veggie soup.

But no matter
what she did, Box
continued to droop.

Then Grace had an idea.

If Box was a sinking boat . . .

maybe she was a peg-leg pirate
trying to keep him afloat!

"Ahoy, matey,
let's try some tape!"

Grace fixed the rip
in his wall.

"Get some cardboard
for reinforcement!"

She patched crumples big and small.

Box looked different now,
but that didn't matter to Grace.

By Monday, he was back to work
as another magical place.

So Box was a fort, then a castle,

which Grace worked
hard defending.

And every few days
a new rip would need
a little mending.

They played the days away
with lots of color and laughter,

because best friends Grace and Box
had big dreams to chase after.

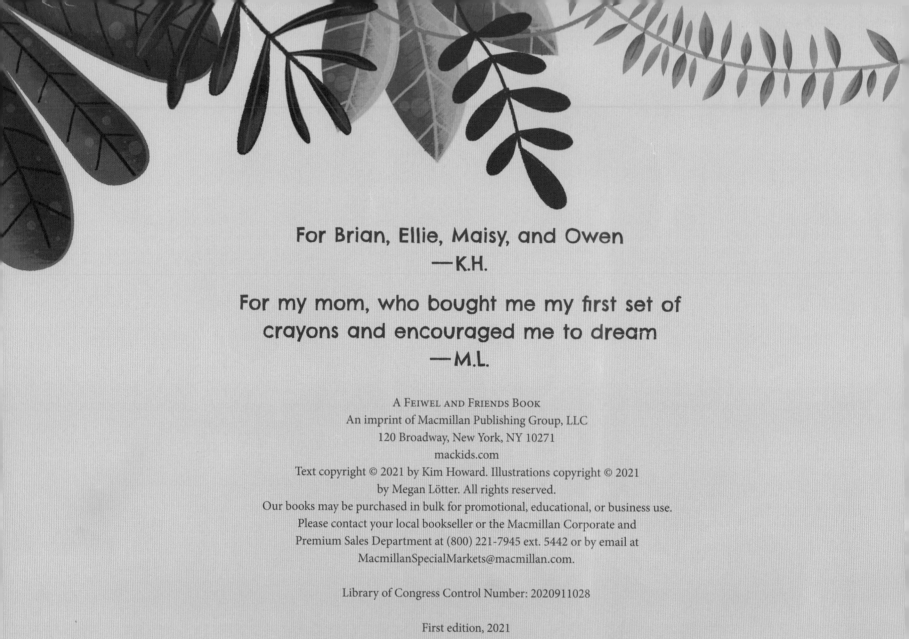

For Brian, Ellie, Maisy, and Owen
—K.H.

For my mom, who bought me my first set of
crayons and encouraged me to dream
—M.L.

A Feiwel and Friends Book
An imprint of Macmillan Publishing Group, LLC
120 Broadway, New York, NY 10271
mackids.com

Our books may be purchased in bulk for promotional, educational, or business use.
Please contact your local bookseller or the Macmillan Corporate and
Premium Sales Department at (800) 221-7945 ext. 5442 or by email at
MacmillanSpecialMarkets@macmillan.com.

Library of Congress Control Number: 2020911028

First edition, 2021
Book design by Mike Burroughs
Printed in China by RR Donnelley Asia Printing Solutions Ltd.,
Dongguan City, Guangdong Province
Feiwel and Friends logo designed by Filomena Tuosto
All illustrations were drawn digitally in Adobe Photoshop.

ISBN: 978-1-250-26294-3
1 3 5 7 9 10 8 6 4 2